For Ady, Annabel, Eli, Juniper, and Levi—good apples, every one.
And for Tara (rock star, ninja), for always believing in the idea of us. —C. S. W.

For my two apples, Calvin and Dylan. Love, Mom. —M. L.

Charlotte Sullivan Wild was a fiscal year 2015 recipient of an Artist Initiative Grant from the Minnesota State Arts Board. The creation of this book was supported by the voters of Minnesota through a grant from the Minnesota State Arts Board, thanks to a legislative appropriation from the arts and cultural heritage fund. She also acknowledges the support of Intermedia Arts, the Jerome Foundation, and the Metropolitan Regional Arts Council of the Twin Cities.

Fist bumps to the Minneapolis students whose insights and joyful dramatizations nurtured this book: the fifth-grade writers of Ascension Catholic School, second-grade poets of Folwell School of Performing Arts Magnet, and readers of Windom Spanish Dual Immersion School. Always wear your magical glasses! —C. S. W.

BLOOMSBURY CHILDREN'S BOOKS

Bloomsbury Publishing Inc., part of Bloomsbury Publishing Plc
1385 Broadway, New York, NY 10018

BLOOMSBURY, BLOOMSBURY CHILDREN'S BOOKS, and the Diana logo are trademarks of Bloomsbury Publishing Plc

First published in the United States of America in February 2019 by Bloomsbury Children's Books

Text copyright © 2019 by Charlotte Sullivan Wild
Illustrations copyright © 2019 by Mary Lundquist

Bloomsbury books may be purchased for business or promotional use. For information on bulk purchases
please contact Macmillan Corporate and Premium Sales Department at specialmarkets@macmillan.com

Library of Congress Cataloging-in-Publication Data
Names: Wild, Charlotte Sullivan, author. | Lundquist, Mary, illustrator.
Title: The amazing idea of you / by Charlotte Sullivan Wild ; illustrated by Mary Lundquist.
Description: New York : Bloomsbury, 2019.
Summary: Illustrations and simple text reveal that there is potential in every seed to be a tree,
in every tadpole to be a frog, and in every child to be a unique and creative adult.
Identifiers: LCCN 2018010845 (print) | LCCN 2018017644 (e-book)
ISBN 978-1-68119-183-6 (hardcover) • ISBN 978-1-68119-184-3 (e-book) • ISBN 978-1-68119-185-0 (e-PDF)
Subjects: | CYAC: Change—Fiction. | Growth—Fiction. | Individuality—Fiction.
Classification: LCC PZ.1.W53213 Am 2019 (print) | LCC PZ.1.W53213 (e-book) | DDC [E]—dc23
LC record available at https://lccn.loc.gov/2018010845

Art created with pencil, watercolor, and gouache on watercolor paper
Typeset in Neutraface Text
Book design by Jeanette Levy
Printed in China by Leo Paper Products, Heshan, Guangdong
2 4 6 8 10 9 7 5 3 1

To find out more about our authors and books visit www.bloomsbury.com and sign up for our newsletters.

The Amazing Idea of You

Charlotte Sullivan Wild • *illustrated by* Mary Lundquist

Peachtree

BLOOMSBURY
CHILDREN'S BOOKS
NEW YORK LONDON OXFORD NEW DELHI SYDNEY

Hidden in this apple

is the idea of a tree

wrapped tight
in this shiny seed.

Take a bite
drop a bit
the idea might take root

sprout
shoot up
into the blue.

And in the nest
curled inside this egg
waits the idea

of a bird . . .

and all the songs
she'll ever sing
for sunrise
or the lapping lake.

And down in the shallows
inside that tadpole
wriggles the idea

of a frog

and a SPRING—
 into green!

And look: the caterpillar
creeping through grass
carries inside

the color and flutter
of a butterfly.

Even those waddling goslings
hold the dream

of whistling flight
over lake and field
through clouds and miles
and days and nights.

Once, someone waited
through nights and days
and the turn of seasons
for the promise
of *you*
curled inside
waiting . . .
to emerge
to open your eyes.

And look at you!
What ideas are hidden
inside of *you*?

A new song
no one has
ever heard?

A springing dance,
fast and free?

The color and swirl
of a painting?

Or the daring to soar
over lake and field
through clouds and sky
as high as you can dream?

Or maybe
on a chilly, drizzly day,
inside you will grow
the idea of something new.
Something alive.
Something for the whole world to share.

So you dig
drop a seed—

dig some more
pat, pat, pat.

You water and sweat
snip, wrap, wrap.

And after blizzards and drizzles
scorches and gales
and all that work
and the long, looooooong wait . . .

. . . you're all grown up.
And look what you've done!

Where you once planted seeds,
    now an *orchard* teems
with creatures singing,
    springing, fluttering, winging—
and people laughing,
    lounging, munching, swinging.

And all around are apples,
apples,
everywhere APPLES.

And every last one
has an idea inside.

Just like you.